cart wheel

chessman

bluebird

cork

crab

candle holder

wrench and grasshopper

sleeping dog

bent saw

crabapple

The King of Little Things

Bil Lepp

Illustrated by David T. Wenzel

PEACHTREE
ATLANTA

To Noah and Ellie,
my little things beginning to happen

—*B. L.*

To Lindsey, my hero

—*D. T. W.*

Published by
PEACHTREE PUBLISHERS
1700 Chattahoochee Avenue
Atlanta, Georgia 30318-2112
www.peachtree-online.com

Text © 2013 by Bil Lepp
Illustrations © 2013 by David T. Wenzel

Acquired by Carmen Agra Deedy
Composition by Loraine M. Joyner

Illustrations were rendered in watercolor on 100% rag archival
watercolor paper. Title and bylines typeset in Microsoft Typography/Font
Bureau's Harrington and Fonts Bomb's Ghost Theory by Abdullah
Alkhafaji, text typeset in International Typeface Corporation's Caxton
by Leslie Usherwood.

Printed in March 2013 by Imago in China
10 9 8 7 6 5 4 3 2 1
First Edition

Library of Congress Cataloging-in-Publication Data

Lepp, Bil, 1970-
  The King of Little Things / text by Bil Lepp ; illustrations by David
Wenzel.
      pages cm
  Summary: "When King Normous decides to become king of the whole
world, the King of Little Things—and his subjects—must find a way to
outsmart Normous and keep their little kingdom safe"—Provided by
publisher.
   ISBN: 978-1-56145-708-3 / 1-56145-708-6
  [1. Kings, queens, rulers, etc.—Fiction. 2. Size—Fiction.] I. Wenzel,
David, 1950- illustrator. II. Title.
  PZ7.L5556Ki 2013
  [E]—dc23
                                            2012032584

LONG AGO, ON THE FAR SIDE of a
mountain, lived the King of Little Things.
While other kings busied themselves with the
big things of this world, he happily ruled over
all things small.

He was king of

coins, candles, combs, keys,
   knots, nods, knobby knees,

bottles, buttons, beetles, burps,
   chiggers, chips, chickadee chirps.

Petals, paddles, paper clips,
   lamp wicks, lentils, lizard lips,

mittens, marbles, macaroni,
   barnacles, bats, and fried bologna.

The King of Little Things had a cozy house
and a loving queen. He fed the birds, left crumbs
for the ants, and planted flowers for the bees.

He had everything he needed, and didn't want for more.

Not so with bigger kings. No matter how vast their kingdoms, they always wanted more: bigger riches, bigger bridges, bigger britches.

Greediest of all was King Normous. He wanted to be king of all the world.

With this in mind, he gathered an army.

A BIG army.

He raided realms.

He squashed sovereignties.

He eradicated empires.

When he was certain he had conquered every

king,

queen,

czar,

empress,

chieftain,

rajah,

and sultan

in the world…

...it was time for some magnificent merrymaking.

He ordered his cooks to fix a fabulous feast.

He commanded his goldsmith to create a colossal crown.

He instructed his tailors to sew a splendid suit.

"At last," proclaimed King Normous as he lifted the glittering crown from its velvet cushion, "I am King of All Things!"

His steward raised a trembling hand.
"I beg your pardon, your Highness
of Great Heft."

"What is it?" snapped the king.

"M-m-my Large Liege," whimpered the steward,
"I believe you may have missed His Minuscule Majesty…
the King of Little Things."

"Little things have a king?" howled Normous.
"What nonsense! Everyone knows that little things
exist only to serve big things."

King Normous stroked his beard. "Where lives this King of Little Things?" he growled.

"Through the old forest, on the far side of a mountain, my Considerable Sire," said his steward.

"Amass my armies!" Normous cried. "We shall go there immediately and put this tiny king in his very small place."

After marching for days, King Normous and his armies
at last neared the land of the King of Little Things.
This would not be a fair fight. And that's just
the way the big king liked it.

As the enemy approached, the King of
Little Things sent a message to his subjects.
He had a plan and he needed their help.

And during the night...
the little things went to work.

The next morning the soldiers found
mealworms in their bread,
chiggers in their underpants,
and fungus between their toes.

Worse yet, there was nothing left to fight with.

Termites had made dust heaps of their arrow shafts.

Water droplets had worked their way into their gunpowder.

And rust had ruined the cannons and catapults.

In a royal rage, King Normous called for his council.

"If we cannot defeat this king through might,"
he roared, "then clearly we must trick him!
We must cheat him. *We must lie.*"

"After all, a lie, no matter how small, is never a little thing." Normous turned to his advisors. "Invite this charlatan to my tent under a flag of truce. *And prepare the dungeon.*"

The instant the King of Little Things entered the tent, small things recognized their master and fell at his feet.

Coins rolled out of the big king's coffers.
Jewels jumped from his crown.
Buttons popped from his suspenders.

Normous stood in his underwear before the entire court.

"Take this puny pretender to the castle!" he shrieked.

"And toss him in the dungeon!"

The soldiers tried. But the dungeon keys were loyal to the King of Little Things and would not turn the lock. The nails recognized their king and sprang from the door to bow before him.

When Normous learned of this, he had the little king taken to the deepest, darkest cavern in the land.

He ordered the entrance
sealed with a stone.

A BIG stone.

Life in the cave was not entirely unpleasant.

Ants brought crumbs.

Birds brought seeds.

Bees brought honey.

But the King of Little Things missed his house.

He missed his garden.

He missed his queen.

He sent a message with the ants, birds, and bees. He respectfully
asked little things everywhere to make themselves known.
The little things loved their king, and they obeyed.

All over the world,
small things began to happen.

Strings unstrung.
Hangers unhung.

Doors closed.
Campfires froze.

Frills unfrilled.
Pickles undilled.

Quills quivered.
Pencils shivered.

Bolts bolted.

Brakes jolted.

Cookies crumbled.

Blocks tumbled.

Ticks and tocks

left their clocks.

Boats listed.

Words twisted.

Lights unlit.

Scarves unknit.

And every little thing,

everywhere,

**REFUSED
TO WORK.**

The people stormed Normous's castle and demanded that he release the prisoner. Abandoned by his armies, the once mighty king had little choice.

So the King of Little Things returned home.

The little things went back to work.

And King Normous?

Ah, well, he spent the rest
of his days looking for

his keys,

his spectacles,

his pocket watch,

his socks,

his wallet,

his hair net…

And he never thought
about little things in the
same way again.

The King of Little Things

watches over many, many small things. Sometimes even he has trouble keeping track of them all. Can you help?

Turn the page and you will see all kinds of little things. How many of them can you find in the book?

There are more little things in the front of the book. Keep searching and find them all.

Good Luck!

jacks and ball

crumbly cookie

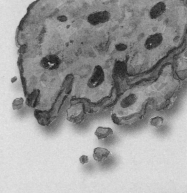

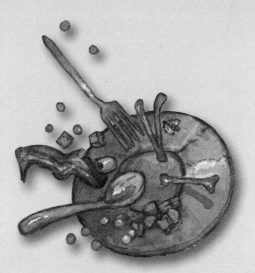

flying plate of food

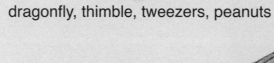

dragonfly, thimble, tweezers, peanuts

frog on lily pad

cat with kittens

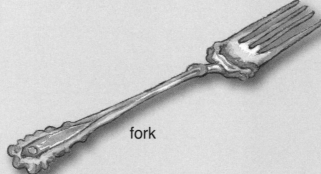

fork

butterfly

crickets

dominoes

mouth harp, harmonica